My Digger is
BIGGER

To Helen: for last minute advice...
and LONG friendship
L.K.

For Claire, Jared, George and Noah,
with love
D.T.

First published in 2017 by Scholastic Children's Books
Euston House, 24 Eversholt Street
London NW1 1DB
a division of Scholastic Ltd
www.scholastic.co.uk
London ~ New York ~ Toronto ~ Sydney ~ Auckland
Mexico City ~ New Delhi ~ Hong Kong

Text copyright © 2017 Lou Kuenzler
Illustrations copyright © 2017 Dan Taylor

PB ISBN 978 1407 17288 0

My Digger is
BIGGER

Lou Kuenzler • Dan Taylor

SCHOLASTIC

Freddie Fox cried, "Hey!
Here comes my **BIG** digger."

Rex Rhino roared, "Crunch!
My digger is...

Orla Ox puffed, "Pah!
My low-loader's so **strong**
It can pull **BOTH** of your diggers along."

"Your loader is **strong**," hissed Anne Anaconda.
"But so is my lorry. It's also much...

"Beep Beep!" brayed Zoe Zebra.

"My car is so **fast**.

If I race with your **lorry**, you will come...

"Vroom! Vroom!"
growled Charlie Cheetah.
"My car is much faster.
My super-fast motor
has a super-charged...

"Bye bye!" buzzed Holly Hornet. "Your car cannot **fly**."
And she **whizzed** in her jet
right up to the . . . .

"Look out!" called Ed Eagle. "I can fly even **higher**".

And his **rocket** roared past with a great **whoosh** of...

As he rocketed by,
Holly Hornet cried, "Wait!
Look out for that space rock!"

But it was too late...

Their boasting and bragging
had caused a huge SMASH!
But little Jack Gerbil avoided the crash.

He picked up his scooter
and without any fuss...

BUS!

Wheeeeeeeeeeeeeeeeeeee!